This book is dedicated to anyone who has ever
owned a smelly, stained, muddy, sticky, painty,
VERY loved blanket ♥
- A M

To Erin, for endless support and helping me
to remember to eat at deadlines
- K A

LITTLE TIGER PRESS LTD,
an imprint of the Little Tiger Group
1 The Coda Centre, 189 Munster Road, London SW6 6AW
www.littletiger.co.uk

First published in Great Britain 2017
Text copyright © Angie Morgan 2017
Illustrations copyright © Kate Alizadeh 2017

A CIP catalogue record for this book is available from the British Library

Printed in China • LTP/1400/1805/0217

2 4 6 8 10 9 7 5 3 1

That is actually MY blanket, Baby!

Angie Morgan • Kate Alizadeh

LITTLE TIGER

LONDON

Once upon a while ago, there was a
brand new baby called Bella,

who had a brand new blanket
called Blanket.

Bella **loved** Blanket.
Everywhere Bella went,
Blanket **HAD** to come too.

Together Bella and Blanket explored the world, and as Bella grew bigger and **bigger . . .**

she grew to love Blanket more and MORE.

Bella and Blanket did **everything** together like painting stuff,

and sticking things to other things,

and **singing** and **dancing** in muddy puddles.

SPLOSH!

Then one day, a brand new baby arrived who had a brand new blanket of his own.

Bella **loved** New Baby.
In fact, she loved him almost as much
as she loved Blanket.

But she thought she would love him
even more if . . .

. . . he didn't **cry** so much.
"Don't cry, Baby," said Bella.
But New Baby went on crying.

So Bella tried
tickling him,

and New Baby
cried —
even
more.

So Bella told
him her very
funniest joke,

but New Baby
didn't laugh
at all.

So Bella showed him her favourite **happy** dance . . .

. . . and New Baby stopped crying.

"That's actually MY blanket, Baby," said Bella. "You have a lovely NEW blanket of your own."

But New Baby didn't want his boring new blanket.
He wanted Bella's sparkly, muddy, painty, smelly one.

"Oh dear," said Bella.
She wasn't at all sure what to do.

So she thought a bit and wondered if . . .

once upon a while ago, Blanket had been all clean and new too.

So she said, "I know, Baby . . ."

"If you take
your clean NEW
blanket . . .

everywhere you go . . ."

"... I will show you how to do stuff like painting, and sticking things to other things,

and singing
and dancing in
muddy puddles."

"And when you have grown
as big as me, Baby,
you will love your blanket
ALMOST as much . . ."

"... as I love you."